CHILLERS

The Haunting of Nadia

JULIA JARMAN

Illustrated by
MICHAEL CHARLTON

PUFFIN BOOKS

CHILLERS

The Blob Tessa Potter and Peter Cottrill
Clive and the Missing Finger Sarah Garland
The Day Matt Sold Great-grandma Eleanor Allen and Jane Cope
The Dinner Lady Tessa Potter and Karen Donnelly
Freak Out! John Talbot
Ghost from the Sea Eleanor Allen and Leanne Franson
Hide and Shriek! Paul Dowling
Jimmy Woods and the Big Bad Wolf Mick Gowar and Barry Wilkinson
Madam Sizzers Sarah Garland
The Mincing Machine Philip Wooderson and Dee Shulman
The Nearly Ghost Baby Delia Huddy and David William
The Real Porky Philips Mark Haddon
Sarah Scarer Sally Christie and Claudio Muñoz
Spooked Philip Wooderson and Jane Cope
Wilf and the Black Hole Hiawyn Oram and Dee Shulman

PUFFIN BOOKS

Published by the Penguin Group
Penguin Books Ltd, 27 Wrights Lane, London W8 5TZ, England
Penguin Putnam Inc., 375 Hudson Street, New York, New York 10014, USA
Penguin Books Australia Ltd, Ringwood, Victoria, Australia
Penguin Books Canada Ltd, 10 Alcorn Avenue, Toronto, Ontario, Canada M4V 3B2
Penguin Books (NZ) Ltd, 182–190 Wairau Road, Auckland 10, New Zealand

Penguin Books Ltd, Registered Offices: Harmondsworth, Middlesex, England

First published by A&C Black (Publishers) Ltd 1997
Published in Puffin Books 1998
3 5 7 9 10 8 6 4 2

Text copyright © Julia Jarman, 1997
Illustrations copyright © Michael Charlton, 1997
All rights reserved

The moral right of the author and illustrator has been asserted

Filmset in Meridien

Made and printed in England by William Clowes Ltd, Beccles and London

British Library Cataloguing in Publication Data
A CIP catalogue record for this book is available from the British Library
ISBN 0–140–38369–7

Chapter One

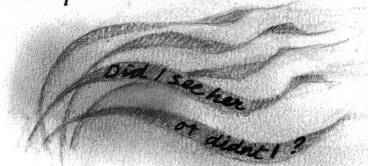

Standing in the school doorway, Nadia wished there was another way home. It was a wet November afternoon, and rain was bouncing off the tarmac. Soon it would be dark, and she didn't want to go past the pond in the dark. She didn't want to go past the pond at all. Jamie Goodband and Matthew Watts rushed by.

They often walked home with Nadia and her friend Julie, but tonight they both had judo club at the community centre.

Matthew grinned
and sped off
after Jamie.

Wishing Julie would come, Nadia gave *herself* a Talking To.

Jenny Greenteeth is an old wives' tale. Jenny Greenteeth is a joke.

It was true. Mothers told their little children, "Don't go near the pond or Jenny Greenteeth will get you!" – and little children laughed.

The pond was in Clophill Road, on a triangle of land between the church and the *Six Ringers*. It was surrounded by trees with dangly branches, and it was covered with green slime.

Algae, Miss Cleverly called it when they had done a project on the pond last term. She remembered Matthew making a joke about it.

There was green algae and sometimes red algae. The red was the blood, people said, of Jenny Greenteeth's victims, after she had dragged them to the bottom with her long stretchy arms, and nibbled them to death with her little green teeth.

Where was Julie? Nadia looked back down the corridor. Walking past the pond wouldn't be so bad with Julie gabbing away. Sometimes, when they were passing she'd shout, "Jenny Greenteeth, are you feeling hungry? Come and eat Jamie and Matthew, will you!"

Did I really see her?

Jenny Greenteeth

hag woman

water witch

Nadia wished she could stop thinking about her.

Chapter Two

Suddenly Julie appeared, her craft apron tied over her head. She ran out into the rain.

Naddy, come on! Stop day-dreaming.

Mrs Hooley, the lollipop lady, was waiting by the zebra crossing. She looked like a deep sea fisherman.

Come on you two! You're the last! But don't run! You could slip on a day like this! And put up your hood, Nadia. You'll get soaked!

She wouldn't let them across till Nadia had covered her hair. To Nadia's relief Julie wanted to run again as soon as they got to the other side. With luck they'd run right past the pond.

But after a few strides, Julie slowed to a walk, and the rain stopped suddenly – about fifty metres from the pond. Nadia could see the *Six Ringers* sign swinging in the wind as Julie started to chat about Jenny Greenteeth.

Jamie Goodband had Romany blood. He was always quoting his granny and telling them stories she'd told him. "She really did have green teeth," said Julie. "Jenny Greenteeth, that is, not his granny!"

Rows and rows of them like a pike and she had green skin and green flowing hair!

Julie loomed at Nadia and went "Oooooh!" expecting her to laugh. But Nadia didn't.

Oooooooh!

By now she could see the white railings
round the pond. She desperately wanted
to cross the road to get further away, but
the traffic was heavy and there was no
stopping Julie who had speeded up again.
She was still talking, but walking ever so
fast at the same time.

Nadia ran to keep up, wishing Julie
would change the subject. But she didn't.

They were nearly there –
would soon be past.
But now Nadia had a
stitch, a really bad stitch!
The pain slowed her down.
Doubled her up.

Julie, wait. I can't go on!

She tried but
she couldn't.

Julie, wait!

Nadia stopped – she had to.
She clung to the white
railing, watching the pond's
green surface as the rain
began to fall again.
But Julie was powering ahead,
and didn't seem to hear.
Nadia tried not to look at the pond,
but she couldn't take her eyes
off the raindrops plinking
into the slime. The water
seemed to bubble. And bulge.

Just like last time.
Just like yesterday.
It was happening again.
The bulge was rising, rising.
Like the dome of a skull.
Draped with green slime.
Sunken eyes stared at her.

Chapter Three

It seemed ages before Julie came. Now she was pulling Nadia to her feet.

They looked back at the pond. Neither of them could see it. "I saw her, Julie. I saw Jenny Greenteeth," said Nadia.

Julie took hold of Nadia's arm, and
muttering about an over-active
imagination, she marched her away from
the pond. "Home! Left, right. Left, right!"
She gave orders and Nadia obeyed like a
zombie.

Jenny Greenteeth wants me
Jenny Greenteeth
wants me

She had seen her twice now.

Jenny Greenteeth wants me

But why? That was the question. *Why?*
Jenny Greenteeth only took bad children.
That's what Jamie's granny said –
disobedient children, liars, cheats and
jealous ones.

"She knows the green-eyes when she
meets them," Granny Goodband said.
"It takes one to know one."

Nadia knew she'd have to go back.

"Left again!" Julie steered her into Cowslip Drive, where they both lived in identical houses. Nadia didn't remember crossing Clophill Road though she knew she must have by the zebra crossing. Julie stopped at Number 34.

"Here we are. This is where you live, Naddy." Julie stared at Nadia searchingly as they stood outside the door. Then she rang the bell and waited till Nadia's mum appeared, with five-year-old Robs at her side. His plump face was beaming, and the hall light behind his golden hair made it shine like a halo.

Oh, hello, Julie!

"Hello, Mrs Toms. Hi, Robs. Er, Naddy's not feeling too well, so I thought I'd see her home safely, but I'd better be off now or my mum'll be in a state." With a last worried glance at Nadia, Julie shot off.

"Naddy!" Robs flung himself at Nadia.

"Come in, love. Quickly now," said Mrs Toms. "Let's get the door closed."

Upstairs, in the warmth and light and pinkness of her bedroom, Nadia thought about what she'd seen. It seemed unreal, like a horror film on the telly. She must have imagined it. As she pulled a sweater over her head, she heard her dad arriving home.

Ever since she was a little girl she'd been able to recognise his footsteps on the path. She heard the door slam and his big voice boom:

Where's my boy?

Here I am!

Nadia stood at the top of the stairs, watching Robs hoisted high in the air – like she used to be.

Who's the King of the castle?

Me! Me! I am!

Of course you are!

No you're not, you're a dirty rascal!

The words came into her head as she watched her dad settle the little boy on his shoulders. It made Nadia feel sick. It was as if a hand squeezed her stomach.

Later, she caught sight of her own face in the mirror. What had her dad said once when he'd noticed her looking like that? "Got a touch of the green eyes, Nadia?"

It takes one to know one

Jenny Greenteeth only took bad children jealous children

Nadia had to admit that she *had* been a bit green-eyed, as her dad called it, before she'd got used to Robs being around.
But she loved him now – adored him.
He was sweet and cuddly and he loved her.
She went downstairs.

23

Robs offered her a chip as they sat down to tea. She ruffled his hair. He really was sweet, the little brother she had always wanted.

"Eat up, Nadia. What's the matter?" said Mum.

She didn't answer. Couldn't. They'd think she was crazy.

"Julie said you weren't well," said Mum.

That night Nadia dreamt that Jenny
Greenteeth was beckoning her with a
flipper hand . . .

. . . drawing her into the
water, deeper and deeper . . .

. . . and binding her with
her long green hair.

When Nadia woke in
the early hours, she
was bathed in sweat
and tangled in bed-
clothes. She knew it
had just been a dream,
but she couldn't get
back to sleep – she
didn't want to.
She lay there
watching the dawn
breaking to another
cold drizzly day.
Then she set off for
school without calling
for the others.

Chapter Four

Jenny Greenteeth was waiting for her.
She was standing at the edge of the pond,
her face half-hidden by her green flowing
hair and the dangling branches of the
willow tree. Her heavy lidded eyes were
unblinking, but one nostril opened and
closed like the mouth of a fish.

*I'm watching you I know your secret
come on in come on in*

Nadia ducked under the railing to get closer – and the hag slid beneath the slime. Where was she? Nadia crouched down and peered into the water.

Nadia moved closer, taking hold of a branch to steady herself. She felt compelled to speak.

I know you're there.

A single bubble
broke the surface.
Then another appeared
nearer the middle. And another.

Then . . . there it was, the bulge of her skull. The sunken eyes.
The bubble from a nostril.

Nadia leaned forward to see the face more clearly.

W-What do you want?

The next moment she felt hands grabbing her, pulling her back. It was Matthew. She tried to fight him off but he wouldn't let go.

She had to finish, had to.

She directed her words to the face in the pond, though more hands were pulling at her. Julie was there and so was Jamie. All three were pulling at her.

But Nadia completed her message,

Only then did she let them haul her on to the pavement. They were looking at her, and then at each other, as if they thought she'd gone mad.

But Nadia wasn't listening.
Something else had caught
her eye – her school bag.
Some of the books and
her dinner pass had
slipped out and the pass
was in the pond, with her
photo facing upwards.
Water had seeped under
the plastic and her hair
was speckled with green.
She looked just like
Jenny Greenteeth.

Jamie fished out the pass with a stick. He took out the photo, wiped it clean, and handed it to Nadia.

Chapter Five

Throughout the day, Julie stuck by Nadia like super-glue. At four o'clock all three friends were waiting to walk home with her. The four of them crossed Clophill Road together well before they got to the pond.

Nadia didn't try to argue. It didn't make any difference. Nor did Jamie's warning. Jenny Greenteeth wanted her. That was enough. She'd go some other time. Probably tonight.

But her mother soon put a stop to that idea when she got home. "I need you to look after Robs for an hour, Nadia," she said. "Your dad and I want to go late-night shopping."

Nadia read Robs stories as she usually did before he went to bed, and he cuddled up to her on the settee, smelling of shampoo and clean pyjamas.

For a while Jenny Greenteeth seemed like a horrible dream.

She carried Robs upstairs and was just putting him into bed when the doorbell rang. It was Julie.

Even before Nadia had got the door open properly Julie said,

I'm not going as that *stupid legend* to the disco, Naddy. It was a daft idea.

"Well if you're not, I will," said Nadia.

Julie looked at her in disbelief.

You're obsessed, Nadia. **Don't**.

Then Robs appeared at the top of the stairs.

"It's a sort of party," said Julie.

"I've been invited to a party," said Robs. Excitedly he rushed to his bedroom and came down holding his invitation.

"It's a smart invitation, Robs," said Julie.

"I've never been to a party before," said Robs. "Tell me about them, please."

While Julie told him about games and nice food and prizes and party bags and fancy dress sometimes, Nadia thought about her costume. Then they both put Robs back to bed. As they walked downstairs, Julie pleaded with Nadia once more.

But Nadia had already made up her mind. As soon as Julie had gone, she started on the costume.

Her swimming costume made a good
base. It was green with the logo NAIAD
on the edge of the leg. That meant water
nymph. So did Nadia. It suited her. She
was good at swimming, and used to go a
lot before Robs was born. Now nobody
had time to take her.

Tomorrow she would go back to the pond
to get some green weed. She wanted to
look exactly like Jenny Greenteeth. She
didn't know why but she did.

But when her parents came in, they
forbade her to go near the pond. "We saw
Mr Carney in town. He said he'd seen
you hanging around the pond," said her
mum. "That's not like you, Nadia, you're
usually so sensible."

I don't want you
to go near the pond
again. It's dangerous.

Nadia went upstairs feeling miserable.
Everyone was trying to thwart her – her
friends and her family.

Chapter Six

All that week Julie, Matthew and Jamie made sure Nadia never walked to or from school on her own, and her mother kept finding things for her to do in the house in the evenings. It wasn't until Saturday morning – the Saturday of the disco and Robs' party – that Nadia got her chance.

Robs was excited and a bit nervous about the party he was going to. It was his friend Craig's birthday. He'd watched Nadia making her costume and decided he must have fancy dress for his party. He went on and on about it.

Please, Naddy, I want a costume, a pirate's costume. Make me a costume. Please.

In the end Nadia agreed to make him one. It wasn't difficult – a white shirt, a cut-off pair of jeans and a handkerchief round his head. But then he wanted a sword. He'd seen a plastic one in the newsagents in Northill.

I must have a pirate's sword. I must have a pirate's sword. Please, Naddy.

Suddenly Nadia saw her chance to visit the pond. Even her mum agreed that Robs could have a sword and said that Nadia could go into Northill to buy one.

On the way back she stopped at the pond. A mist hung over the surface and shrouded the trees. First she checked that there was no one else around. Then she pulled a plastic bag from her pocket and crouched at the water's edge.

Jenny, may I have some of your weed?

She waited, expecting to see the hag
rising from the pond, but the green
surface stayed smooth. There wasn't so
much as a bubble. The water was still and
so were the trees surrounding it. Silence,
that was all. Complete silence. It was odd.
Unnerving. She looked all around. She
looked at the smooth surface. There was
no sign of Jenny Greenteeth. Strange.
She'd felt sure she would see her. She
wanted to see her. To explain what had
happened.

At that, there was a sound – like a sharp intake of breath. It sounded as if it were in the tree behind her, but when she looked, there was nothing there. So leaning forward, she lowered the bag into the water, and dragged it across the surface filling it with weed. Perhaps she didn't need to explain? Perhaps Jenny Greenteeth knew everything?

Chapter Seven

When she got home Nadia spread out the weed on kitchen roll to dry it. Then she took Robs to Craig's party. Craig lived in Bedford Road, four doors away from the school where the disco was being held. Nadia made sure that Robs was happy at the party. He was happy; his pirate costume was much admired.

Then she hurried home to get ready.

The costume was hanging in her wardrobe. She'd spent ages dyeing old tights green and cutting them into long strips and she'd sewn most of them on to her swimming costume but she still had a few more to do.

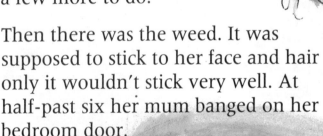

Then there was the weed. It was supposed to stick to her face and hair only it wouldn't stick very well. At half-past six her mum banged on her bedroom door.

Come on, Naddy. I thought we were going to walk to Bedford Road together! You know Dad's got the car.

Nadia didn't answer because she didn't want to move her face muscles – she'd just got some weed to stick. But her mother came in anyway – and stopped dead.

What the... That's horrible! What do you want to look like that for?

Then she remembered the time and said, "That'll have to do, Naddy. Robs will worry if I'm not there on time. You'll just have to come as you are."

Through clenched teeth Nadia muttered,

Go ahead. I'll catch you up.

At first Mrs Toms
didn't understand.

It's dark, Naddy.
I don't like walking
by myself in the
dark, and I don't
like you walking
alone either.

But when she saw that
Nadia wasn't taking
any notice, she gave
up and went down-
stairs. Nadia heard the
doorbell ring. Then she
heard her mum open
the front door.

Hello, Julie, you
look nice. I wish
I could say the
same for Nadia.
She's upstairs. Go
on up. I'm off to
fetch Robs.

Then Julie was standing in the bedroom doorway, dressed as a firebird in bright red, but the colour was leaving her face.

But she glanced in the mirror again – and stepped back as Jenny Greenteeth stared back at her. She had caught her likeness exactly. The taut green skin, the flattened nose – she'd managed that by stretching a nylon stocking over her face. The long hair strewn with weed.

Julie was still in the doorway, chalk-white. Nadia opened and closed her mouth to show Julie her nibbly matchstick teeth.

T-take it off. It's not funny

But Nadia was proud of her creation. She put on her coat and took Julie's arm. Then they both stepped outside into the darkness.

It was bitingly cold. Nadia was glad of her coat and the stocking over her head, which kept the worst of the wind from her ears. On the corner of Cowslip Drive and Clophill Road they met the boys. Jamie and Matthew were both dressed as pirates.

When they saw Nadia, Matthew muttered something about robbing a bank, and managed a laugh, but Jamie looked concerned.

Nobody mentioned Jenny Greenteeth.
Nobody said anything, but they didn't
cross Clophill Road till they were way
past the pond, on the corner of Bedford
Road, where they met Mrs Toms coming
back – without Robs.

Mrs Toms seemed relieved to see Nadia.

At first Nadia thought she hadn't heard properly – disco music was blaring out from the school hall just ahead.

Then suddenly, as Nadia didn't answer, she screamed, "Where's Robs, Naddy?"

And Nadia screamed back,

Mrs Toms circled Nadia as if she thought she might be hiding him. "Craig's mother said you collected him!"

Nadia felt her blood go cold.

Chapter Eight

"Y-you, you were collecting him . . ." she tried to say, but her words were drowned by her mother's jabbering hysterics.

You collected him, Naddy. Mrs Kean said so! She described your stupid costume! How did you get there before me? Did someone give you a lift?

Nadia couldn't move. Terror froze her. Something terrible was happening, something horrifyingly weird. She ought to move. She wanted to move. Robs was in danger. She was sure of it. But her feet were stuck to the pavement. Then she caught sight of Jamie staring at her, looking as horror struck as she was, and she could sense his mind working. Suddenly he grabbed her arm.

They ran. Even before they got to the pond Nadia heard Robs' voice calling her name. "Naddy, where are you?" The street lamp was flickering, shedding its sickly yellow light over the water.

Then she saw him, reaching for his sword which was floating on the surface. She spoke gently so that he wouldn't jump.

He spoke crossly glancing at her, "Where did you go, Naddy? Why did you throw my sword in the pond? Get it back."

No, Robs. We're going home.

Then I'll g....

She reached out to stop him — but he wasn't there!

"He slipped," said Jamie, but there was no sound and no sign. Then, from the pond, came a sucking sound.

"He's gone under," gasped Nadia, plunging her hands into the water, but it was deeper than she thought and thick with weed. She felt all around. Nothing.

In desperation she pushed her head
under the slime – didn't mind the cold,
didn't notice it – and opened her eyes to
search the pond's murky depths. And she
saw something white! A leg? Grabbing it,
she pulled. It seemed to be stuck.

Though desperate for air, she pulled
harder still. And just as she thought she
might have to let go, it budged!

She pulled and pulled, her chest splitting
with pain. She pulled and pulled till
whatever was holding Robs gave way.
Eager hands pulled him on to the bank.

You saved his life.

That was so
brave, Naddy.

Mrs Toms was too shocked to speak.

"You'll get a reward," somebody said.
"A Heart of Gold."

"I don't want a
reward," said Naddy.
She'd got her reward.
Robs was sitting
up coughing and
spluttering and
still holding
his sword.

Soon a police car and an ambulance arrived but it wasn't needed. Nadia told them everything she could. She told the police exactly what she'd seen and heard.

Jamie, Julie, Matthew, Mrs Toms and, later, Craig's mother, all told the police what they had witnessed. The police listened carefully and took notes, but eventually, after further investigations, they found no more witnesses and decided it had all been a misunderstanding.

A week later as Nadia and Julie walked past the pond on their way to school, a council digger was at work. The pond was being filled in.

"So that's the end of that old story," said Julie.

Good riddance.

But was that the end of Jenny Greenteeth? As Nadia stepped over the water sloshing on to the pavement, she couldn't suppress a shiver. If her mother hadn't picked up Robs – who had?